W/D
Staytime.

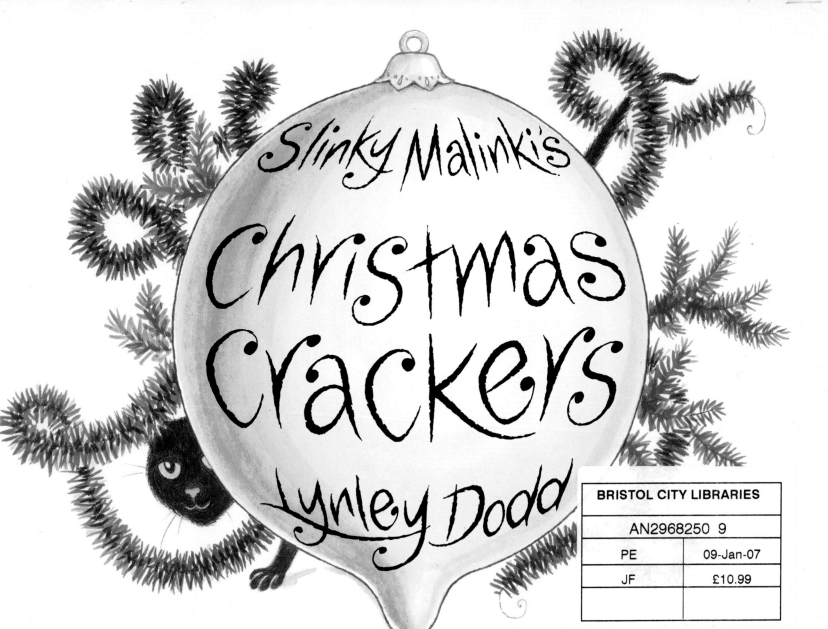

Slinky Malinki's
Christmas Crackers

Lynley Dodd

PUFFIN

Christmas was coming.
Out came the tree,
dressed up in finery
splendid to see.
Trinkets and tinsel
with baubles and bows,
a mouse with a hat
and a very red
nose.

Reindeer and ribbons,
a silvery bell,
glittering stars
and a Santa as well.
Hanging up high
was a lollipop drop,
and the Christmas tree fairy
sat right
at the
top.

Glimmering,
shimmering,
brilliantly bright,
the tree was a truly
MAGNIFICENT
sight.
But . . .
someone was waiting
to meddle and play,
to get up to tricks
in his usual way.

he batted the baubles
and trinkets as well.

The Santa was seized
in a smothery hug,

and the fairy was whisked away
under the rug.

The family said,
'What a GLORIOUS mess!
WE know the culprit –
it's easy to guess.
A bothersome rascal,
a pothersome pain,
Slinky Malinki's been at it –
AGAIN!'

They gathered the tinsel
and fastened the bell,
the baubles,
the trinkets
and reindeer as well.

They hung up the mouse
with the very red nose,
the Santa,
the ribbons
and all of the bows.

'THERE!'
they all said,
as they studied the tree.
'Everything's back
where we meant it to be.
WAIT –
there's a problem,
a serious space –
WHERE IS THE FAIRY?
She's not in her
place!'

They scrabbled and searched
under table and chair,
behind the piano,
and out on the stair.
Under the cushions,
on top of the sill,
but the Christmas tree fairy
stayed hidden
and still.

'Oh FOOZLE!' they said,
'What a shattering shame –
if we haven't a fairy,
it won't be the same.'
Then came a scruffle,
a tinkle of bell,
a wobble of bauble,
a shiver of shell.
Someone said,
'LOOK!
Can you see what I see?'

'THERE is the fairy,
ON TOP
OF THE
TREE!'

PUFFIN BOOKS

Published by the Penguin Group: London, New York,
Australia, Canada, India, Ireland, New Zealand, and South Africa
Penguin Books Limited, Registered Offices: 80 Strand, London WC2R 0RL, England

penguin.com

Published in New Zealand by Mallinson Rendel Publishers Limited 2006
Published in Great Britain in Puffin Books 2006
1 3 5 7 9 10 8 6 4 2
Copyright © Lynley Dodd, 2006
Manufactured in China
ISBN-13: 978−0−141−38303−3
ISBN-10: 0−141−38303−8